SPACE MUTTS

Attack of the Ninja Kittens!

Michael Broad lives in Surrey on Planet Earth, where he writes and illustrates books for children of all ages, including the Jake Cake series, which was shortlisted for the Waterstone's Prize. Michael loves dogs, daydreaming and anything to do with astronomy.

www.michaelbroad.co.uk

Other books by Michael Broad

Spacemutts: Fluffy Assassins from Mars!

MICHAEL BROAD

SPACE MUTTS

Attack of the Ninja Kittens!

MACMILLAN CHILDREN'S BOOKS

First published 2011 by Macmillan Children's Books
a division of Macmillan Publishers Limited
20 New Wharf Road, London N1 9RR
Basingstoke and Oxford
Associated companies throughout the world
www.panmacmillan.com

ISBN 978-0-330-51141-4

1 3 5 7 9 8 6 4 2

A CIP catalogue record for this book is available from
the British Library.

Printed and bound in the UK by CPI Mackays, Chatham ME5 8TD

For Tara

(a wonderful springer spaniel)

The Alien Invasion

Have you ever looked up at the stars and wondered if aliens really exist? Well, they do! Lots of them! All across the galaxy bright green eyes are looking right back at us, studying our world as they prepare to invade it.

Some aliens already walk among us, but they don't have slimy skin or wiggly tentacles. They're cute and fluffy, eat fish and chase mice, and if they're not already living in your home, you've probably seen them in your garden.

That's right – all cats are aliens from outer space! Tiddles from next door is in charge of weapons. Pickle from the post office relays intergalactic orders. And the big ginger tom who lets you tickle his belly on your way to school is an expert in explosives.

It's true that some cats are harmless and happy just being our pets, but if you watch the others closely you'll see they're up to something. Most of them are spies, plotting in secret and preparing for the invasion. Cats have ruled the rest of the galaxy for thousands of years, conquering every habitable world, and now their sights are set on Earth to complete their evil empire.

The feline forces have tried to invade

our planet many times before, which is how so many cats got stranded here. But they were always doomed to fail because Earth is home to the best alien defence force in the universe . . .

THE SPACEMUTTS

When night falls on the Pooch Pound

dogs' home, these courageous canines

board their spaceship and patrol the

galaxy. Man's best friend defending

the Earth against cosmic kitty cats.

THE DOGS

ROCKET Fearless leader
of the Spacemutts

☆

POPPY Plucky pilot of the
spaceship *Dogstar*

BUTCH Inventor, dribbler
and all-round genius

☆

DUKE New recruit
(a shy Great Dane)

THE CATS

LADY FLUFFKINS Evil empress of the entire galaxy (well, almost)

BALDY Cowardly minion of Lady Fluffkins

THE FELINE FORCES Every breed of cat across the galaxy!

Contents

The Gentle Giant

In the Pooch Pound dogs' home, a family were crouching at the bars of the far kennel, gently calling to a large white mound with big black patches. The Great Dane was lying on a blanket with his back to the visitors and, like every other day they had come to meet him, the dog wouldn't budge.

The disappointed family left with the warden, hurrying past three noisy kennels on their way to the door. Butch howled and growled and frothed like a fountain, Poppy bounded in circles snapping at her tail, while Rocket barked as loud as he could. But when the door closed behind the visitors, the room fell silent and the three dogs sniffed the air.

Is it a hamster?

asked Butch, wiping the drool from his mouth.

'No, I don't think so,' said Poppy, poking her nose through the bars to take another sniff.

3

It smells more like a guinea pig, or maybe even a goat!

'A goat?' laughed Butch. 'Humans don't keep goats as pets.'

'They could,' Poppy said uncertainly.

Butch and Poppy looked at Rocket, who had the sharpest nose and was usually the first to list all of the pets the visitors kept at home. Other dogs and cats were easy to identify, but this family smelt of something much more unusual.

I still can't make it out,

said Rocket. The brown
mutt twitched his shiny
black nose and frowned
in concentration.

Though I'm pretty sure
it's something big.

'Not as big as me,' said a deep voice from the far kennel.

The three dogs turned to Duke, the shy Great Dane.

The gentle giant had arrived at the Pooch Pound a week ago when his family decided he was too large to manage. Duke had been returned to the Pooch Pound many times before for the same reason and this had made him very conscious of his size.

'Whatever pets the family have, they obviously want to give you a home too,' said Poppy, gazing up as Duke heaved

himself to his full height. 'They've come to see you every day this week – maybe you should give them a chance.'

'But I'll bump into their furniture and break things without meaning to,' Duke sighed, lowering his head. 'I don't want

them to be cross with me like all the other families, so I'm staying here where I won't be any trouble.'

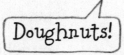

slobbered Butch.

Rocket and Poppy frowned at their kennel mate.

'I can *smell* doughnuts,' Butch added, dribbling on the floor. 'Which means the night warden has arrived, so no one else will be in here until morning rounds!'

Rocket tilted his head and twitched his ear, then he nodded to Butch and Poppy that it was time to leave. The three dogs quickly bunched up their blankets, cleared away chew toys and took up positions in the middle of their kennels, directly beneath the light. Duke watched through the bars, knowing that the Spacemutts would soon be off on another intergalactic adventure.

'Are you sure you won't come with us?' asked Poppy, aware that the Great Dane had declined their offer every other night and probably wouldn't change his mind.

'There's lots of space in space,' added Butch.

Duke smiled, but slowly shook his head. He wished he were brave enough to join his friends – to travel through the galaxy defending the Earth against feline foes. But he felt much too big and clumsy and was sure he would only get in their way.

Rocket swiped his collar with a paw, which made the chrome spikes light up round his neck. 'This is Rocket calling the *Dogstar*,' he said. 'Come in, *Dogstar*.'

'Hello, Captain,' said the female voice of WOOF, the spaceship's onboard computer. 'Everything is prepped for

boarding. Can I confirm only three teleports again this evening?'

Rocket looked over at the fourth kennel where the Great Dane stretched his hind legs and gave a long, low groan. The captain knew big dogs needed lots of exercise and wondered if an adventure with the Spacemutts could also give Duke the confidence he needed to trust a new family.

'Captain?' WOOF repeated, waiting for the command.

'Make that *four* teleports,' whispered Rocket. 'Over and out.'

Moments
later the domed
lights began to
flicker in the
kennels and
four bright beams
shot down from the
ceiling. Spotting the extra
teleport, Poppy and Butch
smiled at Rocket – while
Duke paused
mid-stretch
and gazed up
with a gulp.

'WHOOOOHH . . .' he protested, and the four dogs sparkled in the light as they vanished within the transport beams, leaving all of the kennels empty.

SPACEMUTTS

At the edge of the galaxy in the Catnip Nebula, Lady Fluffkins sat on the bridge of her clockwork *Mouseship* and hissed at planet Earth through her intergalactic telescope.

The white Persian was devising a new fiendish plot to invade the blue planet and thereby complete her empire, but a rattling-chattering sound had disturbed her wicked thoughts, making her glance around irritably.

Is that you making a racket?

she
demanded,
green eyes glaring
at her hairless
servant, Baldy. He was cowering next
to Lady Fluffkins' throne and shaking
more than usual.

'Y-y-yes, m-m-mistress,' he stammered,
bones rattling and teeth chattering.

'Really?' sniffed the empress. 'I hadn't noticed.'

'That's because you are wrapped in the most b-b-beautiful fluffy fur,' snivelled the servant, aware that Lady Fluffkins' vanity ranked much higher than his own well-being. 'While I am . . .'

'A hairless freak?' purred the Persian. 'Yes, you are. And your jangling carcass is disturbing my thoughts. I suggest you either learn how to grow fur or fix the heating, before I toss you out of the air-lock!'

Baldy quickly scuttled away, rubbing

his stringy tail to warm it as he checked the control panels of the clockwork *Mouseship*. Power levels were critically low across all systems, so he peered through the side portal to find that the giant key had stopped turning.

'The clockwork k-k-key has wound down, m-m-mistress,' he shivered.

'Then wind it up again, you bald buffoon!' growled Lady Fluffkins, lazily stroking her thick white coat. 'Or are you suggesting that *I* go out there and get ice crystals on my delicious downy fur?'

A Sitting Duck

The *Dogstar* orbited planet Earth like a great metal tank. Inside the spaceship, four teleport beams appeared upon the deck, followed by four sparkling dogs. As the beams dropped away, the three regular Spacemutts and the reluctant new recruit were greeted by an alert siren!

WOOooOOF!

WOOooOOF!

WOOoooOOF!

Poppy immediately leapt to the cockpit and switched the *Dogstar* controls from autopilot to manual, while Butch dashed away to inspect the mechanics at the rear of the ship. Rocket bounded over to the central hub to silence the alarm and then flicked on the giant screen.

'What have you got for us, WOOF?' he asked.

WOOF was short for World Orbiting
Observation Facility. The ship's computer
constantly scanned the galaxy for
unusual activity, analysing

data from spy-bone satellites and deep-space telescopes.

'I've just picked up an audio pulse in the Catnip Nebula, Captain,' said WOOF, displaying a galaxy map that marked the exact location and feeding the sound through the ship's speakers. 'Its irregular thumping indicates the presence of a life form!'

'Can you get a visual?' asked Rocket, frowning at the strange sound.

'Negative, Captain,' said WOOF, zooming in on the map and switching the view to include local planets. 'And the object is giving off no heat for thermal-imaging.'

It sounds like clanging metal,

said Rocket, twitching his ears.

Fluffkins could be rattling a fork inside a giant tin of tuna,

said Butch, and dribbled on the floor.

'Or she could be *building* something,' Poppy said gravely.

Studying the image on the screen, the captain of the Spacemutts scratched his ear with a rear paw as he considered their options. Lady Fluffkins' distant realm was a dangerous place for dogs, but if the evil empress was building something that threatened planet Earth, they definitely needed to know about it.

'Butch, prep the ship for a wormhole jump to the Catnip Nebula,' said Rocket, rolling out a star map that showed local portals for deep-space travel. 'Poppy, we're going on a scouting mission.'

'Yes, Captain,' said Butch and Poppy together, and set to work.

'Duke, you can . . . ' Rocket glanced up at the empty transportation deck and then scanned the ship to find the Great Dane slumped in a corner. 'Er, you can sit this one out if you like.'

'Yes, Captain,' groaned Duke, certain that his size was a hazard on a spaceship filled with so much technical equipment. So he decided to keep his head down and stay out of the way.

When Butch had completed the engine preparations, Rocket sent coordinates to Poppy, who steered the *Dogstar* through a bright swirling portal located behind Earth's moon.

'WOOOO HOOOO!' cheered the Spacemutts as they shot through a tunnel of rainbow light that looped and curved wildly, spiralling through the galaxy. The dogs howled with joy at the incredible speed, noses forward and ears flapping on the side of their heads.

The wormhole jump was a rollercoaster ride through space and time, but the

journey
was
over in the
shake of a tail
and moments
later the *Dogstar*
burst through the exit
portal in the Catnip Nebula.

In a flurry of movement Poppy hit the brake jets, Butch cut the engines and Rocket shut down the ship's computer, leaving only basic functions running as the *Dogstar* coasted silently through enemy territory. The Spacemutts then gathered at the cockpit and peered out into the Catnip Nebula. The vast red gas-cloud twinkled with distant stars as they passed through a minefield of small local planets.

'I can hear the pulse,' said Rocket, tilting his head and twitching his ears.

The Captain then darted away and leapt on to the central hub, where he pulled down the periscope and scanned the skies until he located the source.

'GRRRR!' he growled, transferring the image to the giant screen.

Butch and Poppy joined Rocket at the hub, and even Duke lifted his head as the image flickered into view. It showed the

clockwork *Mouseship* tumbling through space with a shivering Baldy clinging to the top. The hairless servant was making a constant racket as his chilly paws grappled with the key.

'*That* was the pulse?' said Rocket. 'Baldy banging on the ship?'

'It's too easy,' said Poppy. 'It has to be a trap!'

'The *Mouseship* appears to be completely without power,' said WOOF, scanning the systems of the clockwork craft. 'Which is why I could not identify its electronic signature.'

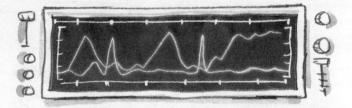

'A sitting duck!' drooled Butch.

This might be our chance to capture Lady Fluffkins once and for all!

said Rocket, wagging his tail excitedly. 'And when she's safely in our custody, planet Earth will finally be safe from the feline forces!'

'But how will we get to her?' asked Poppy.

The Spacemutts thought hard. A Space Walkies to the *Mouseship* was the obvious choice, but with Lady Fluffkins waiting for them inside it was far too dangerous to attempt.

'The Cheese Magnet!' declared Butch.

'Huh?' said Rocket and Poppy together.

Butch bounded to the back of the ship and returned wheeling a large crane with a fishing reel attached to the base. Dangling from the line at the other end was a holey metal wedge that looked like a lump of cheese. Butch swept the dust from the contraption and patted it proudly.

said Rocket and Poppy again.

'I invented the Cheese Magnet to fish for the *Mouseship* in outer space,' Butch

explained. 'Unfortunately the line was too short for it to work long-distance, but we can use it to reel her in through the cargo doors!'

'Bring the *whole ship* aboard the *Dogstar*?' gasped Poppy.

'Actually, it makes sense,' said Rocket, pacing up and down. 'Once Fluffkins is inside she won't be able to escape. Then all we have to do is get her into the maximum-security cat basket!'

3

Planet Puss

The Cheese Magnet shot out through the
Dogstar's rear cargo doors and drifted
towards the *Mouseship*, landing with a
CLUNK! on its shiny black nose. Baldy
quickly clung to the key as the clockwork

craft was reeled in to the
docking bay, and then
held on even tighter

when he peered down at three familiar Spacemutts and one giant dog.

With the docking bay secured, Rocket approached the metal door of the *Mouseship*, put down the maximum-security cat basket and was joined by Poppy and Butch. The Captain then

nodded to his crew and hit
the external door-release
with a paw.

The Spacemutts were
prepared to pounce as the door dropped
down, but the ship was pitch black inside
and nothing moved or made a sound.

SPACEMUTTS

Rocket frowned at his crew and then slowly padded up the steps to board the enemy craft.

Deep in the darkness, two green eyes flicked open.

'YEEEEEAAAAAWWWW!' screamed a white ball of fur as it shot from the

Mouseship, paws briefly landing on Rocket's head as a springboard to freedom.

SPACEMUTTS

In a blur of movement, Lady Fluffkins raced along the curved walls of the *Dogstar*, darting back and forth as the Spacemutts chased after her. Duke was too big to join in so he hid inside the *Mouseship*, while Baldy watched everything from the safety of the clockwork key.

The Persian shot around the *Dogstar* like a hissing ball of lightning, always a whisker away from the barking Spacemutts. Lady Fluffkins knew she was trapped and would

be caught
eventually,
so her sharp eyes
studied the *Dogstar*
controls each time
she whizzed past
the cockpit.

Once she'd gathered all the infor-
mation she needed, the empress darted
up the nose of the *Mouseship*, snatched
Baldy from the key and threw him at the
dogs. This gave her just enough time to

put her plan into action. While Rocket, Poppy and Butch ducked to avoid the yowling servant, Lady Fluffkins back-flipped over their heads and landed in the pilot seat of the *Dogstar*.

'NOOOOO!' howled the Spacemutts as Fluffkins used all four of her snowy white paws to cut the autopilot, ignite the turbojets and plunge the steering levers down.

The result was a rapid nosedive at

incredible speed that threw the ship into zero gravity. The empress quickly dug her claws into the padded pilot seat and cackled wildly, glancing back with glee as the Spacemutts tumbled around the ship.

While Poppy and Butch spun through the air, Rocket flipped himself upright and peered through the observation window.

UH OH!

he barked when he saw that they were hurtling towards a small pink planet!

The captain knew he couldn't pull the *Dogstar* out of the nosedive before they crashed, but he could still capture Lady Fluffkins. The maximum-security cat basket was floating nearby, so he snatched it in his mouth and doggy-paddled with all his might towards the cockpit.

The *Dogstar* burst through the atmosphere of the pink planet and plummeted through the clouds, its bolted panels creaking and groaning while the interior rattled angrily. Rocket could see the alien landscape rapidly approaching and made one final leap towards the empress.

In the pilot seat, Lady Fluffkins was looking straight ahead and bracing herself for a bumpy landing – so she shrieked with alarm when a brown paw grabbed her fluffy tail, stuffed her into a wicker basket and slammed the bars across the front.

Moments later the *Dogstar* hit the ground at high speed and bounded along the peculiar pink terrain, eventually landing in a battered heap at the base of a diamond mountain.

✩

Rocket awoke with a groan and opened his eyes to see the worried faces of Poppy and Butch peering down at him. Butch looked like he might dribble at any moment so the captain quickly leapt up and scanned the battered *Dogstar*.

'How long was I unconscious?' he gasped.

'We don't know,' said Poppy. 'The

impact knocked us all out cold.'

'The *Mouseship* is gone and Duke is missing,' said Butch, nodding towards the open cargo doors and the tracks leading out into the strange pink landscape. 'Fluffkins and Baldy must have kidnapped him while we were all snoozing.'

Rocket frowned and began sniffing around the ship with his nose to the floor, following a scent to the transportation deck. There he nudged away fallen maps and charts and uncovered the maximum-security cat basket with Baldy cowering behind it.

'Fluffkins can't
have done
it,' said the
captain,
as Poppy
and Butch
joined him
and peered
through
the bars. The
empress was snoring
on her back with her paws in the air.
'Which means someone else has taken
the *Mouseship* and Duke along with it!'

Suddenly the giant screen above the hub flickered on and the Spacemutts looked up to see a sleek pink cat sitting on a large diamond throne. Beside the throne sat an embarrassed Great Dane with a thick chain round his neck.

'I am Princess Puss and this is my planet,' purred the cat, patting Duke on the head with a playful paw. 'And I believe I have something that belongs to you.'

'If you harm one hair on his head . . . ' growled Rocket, bounding over to the central hub.

'I have no plans to harm the dog,' interrupted the princess. 'I only took the *Mouseship* because I thought my sister was inside. You can imagine my surprise when I found this big brute cowering in the corner!'

Lady Fluffkins is your sister?

asked Poppy.

'Yes, but we don't get on,' hissed the cat. 'I haven't seen her since we were kittens. That's when she started building armies to rule the galaxy and set her sights on planet Earth. She's quite mad, you know.'

We know,

mumbled Butch.

'Anyway, I would like to propose a little exchange,' said Princess Puss. 'Lady Fluffkins for the brute, and I promise to imprison the empress in a diamond tower where she won't be a nuisance to anyone.'

'And I suppose *you'll* rule the galaxy in her place,' growled Rocket.

'Naturally,' purred the cat. 'But I have no interest in your planet.'

'Why should we trust you?' Rocket demanded, jumping up to the hub so his head drew level with the screen. 'How do we know you won't just keep us here and order the feline forces to invade Earth?'

'Because it's entirely the wrong colour,' hissed the cat. 'Earth is blue, and I only like things that are pink. PINK! PINK! PINK!' she squealed, slamming her paws on the armrests of her throne.

'And if we don't agree to the exchange?' asked Rocket.

'Then I will set you all to work in my diamond mines,' sniffed Puss.

The captain glanced at his crew while he considered their position, then he flattened his ears and turned back to the screen. 'Where do you want the exchange to take place?' he growled.

Princess Puss gave the captain directions to a place called Magenta Forest and then abruptly ended the transmission. When the screen went blank, Rocket hopped down to discuss the situation in a huddle with the Spacemutts.

Meanwhile, in the cat basket on the transportation deck, Lady Fluffkins' snores were becoming snorts and snuffles as she slowly began to wake.

Spiky Ninja Kittens

'I trust Princess Puss about as much as I trust Lady Fluffkins,' said Rocket. 'She's a cat first and foremost, which means she's probably lying through her whiskers.'

Poppy and Butch nodded in agreement.

'But we're not leaving this planet without Duke,' the captain added firmly. 'There's a family waiting for him back

on Earth, and I want to see that big dog settled in a happy home.'

'We can't hand over the empress,' said Poppy.

'And the pink pompom is expecting a swap,' said Butch.

'What a pickle you're in!' hissed a voice from the transportation deck.

The Spacemutts turned to see two green eyes glaring at them through the bars of the cat basket. Lady Fluffkins was picking her teeth with a long, sharp claw and grinning at her captors.

'What we need is a decoy to trade in her place!' said

Rocket, ignoring the empress to focus on the problem at hand. 'Princess Puss said she hasn't seen her sister since they were kittens, so she probably won't remember exactly what she looks like . . .'

'A decoy!' scoffed Fluffkins. 'HA! HA! HA!'

'What's so funny?' barked Poppy.

'My sister may not be very bright,' said the Persian, looking very pleased with herself, 'but I'm fairly certain she knows I'm not a fleabag dog, and I don't see any other cats around here.'

'There is *one* other cat aboard this ship,'

said Rocket, bounding on to the deck. He nudged Baldy out from his hiding place behind the cat basket and frowned. 'He's about the right size too.'

'HA! HA! HA!' laughed the empress, looking the hairless servant up and down with a sour expression on her furry face. 'I know dogs are stupid, but even *you* must have spotted a tiny flaw in your plan.'

'Not really,' said the captain, returning to his crew.

Rocket exchanged a few words with the Spacemutts, who nodded and looked from Lady Fluffkins to Baldy and back again. Then Poppy and Butch tried their best not to smirk as the captain trotted away to the rear of the ship.

Inside the maximum-security cat basket, the evil empress knew something was going on and narrowed her eyes at Baldy. The quivering servant had seen this look before – it meant whatever was about to happen would be entirely his fault.

When Rocket
returned he had
something shiny
in his mouth.
The empress
couldn't make
out exactly
what it was,
but when Poppy
and Butch took
up positions on either side of the basket
and opened the cage door, she backed
into the corner with her hackles up and
hissed loudly.

Lady Fluffkins' hiss was quickly drowned out by an even louder BUZZ as Rocket flicked on the doggy hair-clippers and poked his head through the wicker archway.

☆

'You'll never get away with this!' spat the empress, eyes glowering from the shadows of her wicker prison as the Spacemutts prepared a newly fluffy Baldy for the hostage exchange. 'I'll have you all stuffed and mounted on the wall of my kitty-litter room!'

Lady Fluffkins had been delivering a

steady stream of threats while the dogs gathered up tufts of her fur and stuck them on to Baldy's skinny body, though her vanity kept the empress hidden in the shadows.

When the dogs had finished, the servant looked like a tatty white cat. He was still bald in places, but as Poppy moved round him with a mirror the Spacemutts all agreed that the main bits were covered.

Baldy gasped when he caught a glimpse of his own reflection and, forgetting himself entirely, stroked his new fur lovingly with a paw. It was only when he turned to flick his fluffy tail playfully that he saw his mistress watching him.

'Well, look at *you* all dressed up,' growled Lady Fluffkins, stalking up to the bars and into the light. Her coat was now short and patchy with a few tufts of long hair sprouting from her head. 'So *very* pretty at my expense.'

Baldy swallowed hard and was about to beg for forgiveness when Rocket announced that it was time to leave and quickly ushered him

outside the ship. Butch and Poppy then followed close behind, closing the cargo doors on the seething empress.

'Now, you know what you have to do,' Rocket said to Baldy as they made their way across a pink landscape studded with diamond mountains, towards Magenta Forest. 'Just act all snooty and don't say a word.'

Baldy nodded, though he was much more concerned about the wrath of his mistress than what the

dogs would do if he disobeyed them. The Spacemutts were the enemy, but Lady Fluffkins would be much more terrifying if she ever escaped from her prison.

☆

Magenta Forest was a sprawling mass of spindly trees with puffy pink tops like candyfloss. Rocket stayed up front as they headed for the exchange point,

while Poppy and Butch guarded the fake Lady Fluffkins.

When the strange trees eventually thinned out, the Spacemutts stepped into a clearing to find Princess Puss waiting for them. Duke was nowhere to be seen, and as the dogs moved forward, the bushes rustled around them.

They had walked right into a trap!

Princess Puss grinned at the Spacemutts as an army of black ninja kittens sprang from the bushes, kicking and punching the air as they surrounded the dogs on all sides. The kittens were not very big, but they were armed with swords and daggers made from sharp diamond shards.

'Where's Duke?' Rocket demanded.

'You expect me to keep my end of the bargain when you bring me that monstrosity?' laughed Princess Puss, frowning at the scruffy servant who was peeping out from behind Poppy and Butch.

'We still have Fluffkins,' said the captain.

'Are you sure about that?' smiled Princess Puss.

The captain quickly swiped his collar, making the chrome spikes glow around his neck. 'This is Rocket calling the

Dogstar,' he whispered. 'WOOF, can you give me a status report?'

'The cargo doors have been breached, Captain,' said WOOF. 'The ninja kittens arrived soon after you left. I tried to keep them out, but they swarmed on to the ship and somehow managed to cut through my security circuits.'

'And the empress?' asked Rocket, already knowing the answer.

'Gone,' said WOOF.

'Diamonds,' chuckled Princess Puss, fanning herself with a lazy pink paw. 'They really are a girl's best friend because

they can cut through anything. Metal, wires – even the bars of a maximum-security cat basket!'

'So where is she?' growled Rocket, stalling for time while he worked out how to hurdle the huddle of spiky ninjas and get back to the ship. 'I've never known Lady Fluffkins pass up a chance to gloat.'

'Oh, I think I hear her now,' said the cat, sitting up and tilting her head at the sound of distant trotting. 'After having such a bad hair day, my sister insisted on a dramatic entrance.'

The Spacemutts all looked up as Duke

slowly appeared through the trees. The Great Dane was wearing a harness and saddle, and perched upon his back was Lady Fluffkins in a fluffy cape, a matching fluffy hat and long black riding boots.

5

Diamond Dogs

'Gee up, you big oaf!' huffed Lady Fluffkins, tugging roughly at the reins as Duke plodded into the clearing and stopped beside Princess Puss. The Great Dane's head hung low with shame when he saw his trapped friends.

Rocket immediately bounded forward to rescue Duke, but the spiky kittens closed ranks round the Spacemutts, penning them in with a menacing MEEEOW! The dogs snarled at the kittens, darting back and forth in the circle of spines, but they were as sharp as needles and too high to jump.

'This is all my fault,' Rocket whispered to Butch and Poppy. 'If I hadn't tricked Duke into coming along, that big dog would still be fast asleep in a nice warm kennel.'

'But he would never have trusted another human,' said Poppy. 'And I know that's why you brought him along, to give him a chance to prove himself and gain some confidence.'

'Maybe I expected too much of him,' sighed Rocket.

'Duke could see off both of those mean cats *and* their army of prickly kittens!'

said Butch. 'If only there was some way to get through to him, give him something to fight for.'

'He has a family waiting back home,' said Rocket, recalling the scent of the humans and how they kept coming back, just to see Duke. 'If only we could persuade him to give them a chance.'

While the dogs were distracted, Baldy saw his chance and shot away through a small gap in the kitten enclosure. He crept towards his mistress and peered up at her with pleading eyes.

M—M—M MISTRESS?

he stammered, through fear rather than cold.

'I'll deal with you later,' sniffed the empress, her attention remaining fixed on the trapped Spacemutts. Nudging Duke forward, Lady Fluffkins peered down at the pacing dogs from her massive mount, delighting in their frustration.

'Your plan was a wicked work of genius, sister,' said Princess Puss, grovelling before the empress. 'Only you could have conceived such a complicated and daring plot.'

'It was risky stranding the *Mouseship* in space without power,' agreed the empress, making sure the Spacemutts could hear her. 'But the dumb dogs took a little walkies right into my trap . . . '

'You *planned* all this?' growled Rocket.

'Yes,' hissed Lady Fluffkins, tugging

the cape round her neck. 'Everything except the haircut which, I admit, was a little unfortunate. But a small price to pay now that Earth is finally mine for the taking.'

'Duke, we need your help!' said Rocket.

'You're the only one who can do it!' pleaded Poppy.

'Think of all the lovely food back home!' drooled Butch.

The Great Dane glanced up at his friends, but then sighed heavily and lowered his head again. Duke wanted to help the Spacemutts more than anything, but he lacked the courage to even try.

'HA! HA! HA!' laughed Lady Fluffkins, bouncing up and down in the saddle and kicking her boots with glee. 'You really think this spineless oaf can help you?'

'I know he can,' growled Rocket. 'He just needs to believe that Earth is worth saving, and that there are humans who will love him if he'll only give them a chance.'

'Nice try,' spat the empress, drawing a riding crop from her boot and tapping Duke on the head with it. 'But this one

has no fight in him
whatsoever, which is
why I plan to keep
him as my own
personal pony!'

Rocket was
about to snarl at
the empress, but
frowned instead.

'Ponies,' he
whispered,
looking from
Poppy to Butch
and back again

with excitement. 'That's the scent I couldn't place in the kennels. The family that have been visiting Duke keep ponies – lots of them!'

'Which means loads of lovely sugar lumps,' Butch said, dribbling.

'No,' gasped Poppy, looking up at the shy Great Dane and smiling when she saw his ear twitch. 'It means stables and fields and woodlands for riding!'

'Wide open spaces with nothing to break . . . ' said Duke, lifting his head.

'Poppycock!' snapped Lady Fluffkins, swishing her crop back and forth to keep her balance as the Great Dane shifted beneath her. 'They're lying. No one wants a big ugly beast like you!'

'YES, THEY DO!' Duke growled firmly, nodding at the captain.

Rocket nodded back and gathered Poppy and Butch together, then the Spacemutts watched with pride as the Great Dane took a deep, confident breath and drew himself up to his full height.

'Get down!' Fluffkins demanded, lifting the crop to whip the dog.

Duke turned his head and snatched the riding crop so fast that the empress didn't have time to let go and dangled on its end below the Great Dane's jaws. Then the Persian's green eyes widened as Duke flicked his massive head and sent her flying through the air.

'YEEEEEEEEOOOOW!' shrieked Lady Fluffkins, cape flapping angrily as she plummeted back down again, heading straight for Princess Puss.

Duke ignored the screeching sisters and leapt over the ninja kittens' swords, scooping up each of the Spacemutts and placing them on his back. Then he bounded back through Magenta Forest, heading for the *Dogstar*.

'After them, you fools!' squealed Princess Puss, hissing at the kittens as she wriggled out from under her sister to follow the ninja posse. 'If we fail the

empress now, she will *never* honour us again!'

Baldy was suddenly left alone with Lady Fluffkins, who was still tangled in her cape and trying to claw her way out, spitting and cursing for someone to assist her. He held his breath as he watched the ball of fury, and then slowly crept away to find somewhere safe to hide. The servant only made it a short way before the heel of a riding boot landed firmly on his tail.

'And where do you think *you're* going?' hissed a familiar voice.

Baldy turned his tatty head to see Lady Fluffkins glaring down at him, her shredded cape flapping in the breeze. She leant forward and drew the doggy hair-clippers from her boot.

'I believe you still have something that belongs to me,' said the Empress, green eyes flaring beneath her crooked hat. 'And I intend to take it back.'

Rocket's sharp ears caught the distant BUZZ of clippers as the Spacemutts bounded towards the *Dogstar*'s open cargo

doors, but he was far more concerned about the HISS of approaching ninjas, so he swiped his studded collar.

'WOOF, prep the ship for take-off!' he barked.

'Yes, Captain,' said WOOF, and fired up the engines.

The *Dogstar* was already hovering above the ground when the dogs arrived and bounded in the back, skidding along the metal floor. The cargo doors then closed on the leaping kittens and the battered ship soared away from the pink planet, heading for home.

Family and Furry Friends

Back in the Pooch Pound dogs' home, Duke was still thrilled about his intergalactic adventure, and the Spacemutts enjoyed seeing the Great Dane filled with so much excitement.

I've never run so fast in all my life!

gasped Duke, circling his cage as he recalled the chase. 'It was the most brilliant feeling to have so much open space!'

You'll have that all the time with your new family,

said Poppy.

And don't forget the endless supply of sugar lumps!

slobbered Butch, licking his lips before he dribbled on his blanket. 'They'll come in very handy if you ever run out of energy.'

The Great Dane stopped pacing and looked back at the Spacemutts.

'Though maybe I should stay here after all,' he frowned. 'You might need a big dog like me in your battles against the feline forces. Who knows what Lady Fluffkins will come up with next?'

'I don't think that kennel is big enough for you any more,' said Rocket, aware that Duke had not sat down since the teleport beamed them home. 'Anyway, you've saved the Earth once already.'

'And you can keep an eye on the wild cats that roam the countryside,' said Poppy. 'I'm told they often gather in groups, so we need you to keep an eye on them and make sure they don't build an army here on Earth.'

'I will,' said Duke, and for a moment he seemed sad again.

'What's up?' asked Butch.

'I'm looking forward to having a family again, and it's only because you all believed in me,' said the Great Dane, shifting awkwardly. 'I just wish you could all find new homes too.'

'We will one day, when we finally capture Lady Fluffkins,' said Rocket, nodding to Poppy and Butch when he heard

121

footsteps approaching. 'Meanwhile, friends like you are our family, as well as any new recruit who takes your kennel when you leave.'

The door to the kennels suddenly opened and the warden led a pony-scented family past the three noisy kennels to the one at the end. Through all the dribbling, circling, barking bad behaviour that kept them in the Pooch Pound, the Spacemutts could hear sighs of delight from the humans as Duke eagerly adopted them.

The Great Dane soon left the kennels

with his head held high, confident that his new family would love him for the big dog that he was. And as he passed each of his friends, he hoped it wouldn't be too long before they found happy homes too.

Maybe next time . . .

SPACEMUTTS GALAXY GRAND SLAM GAMEPLAY

The more collector cards, the better the game!

To begin a new game, all cards are dealt face down between two or more players. The dealer then takes the topmost card from their pile and chooses a category to do BATTLE with the other player(s).

There are six categories, SIZE, BRAINS, SKILL, SPEED, CUNNING and STRENGTH, and each character has varying abilities. A small cat will obviously lose against a big dog in a BATTLE of SIZE but could triumph in a BATTLE of CUNNING, so choose wisely.

The challenger reads out the number from their chosen category and the other player(s) reveal their score(s) from the same category. The player with the highest number wins the BATTLE, and all cards played in that round go to the bottom of their pile.

The winner of each BATTLE takes the next topmost card from their pile to begin a new round, and the ultimate GALAXY GRAND SLAM winner (and RULER OF THE ENTIRE GALAXY!) is the player left holding all of the cards.

A selected list of titles available from Macmillan Children's Books

The prices shown below are correct at the time of going to press. However, Macmillan Publishers reserves the right to show new retail prices on covers, which may differ from those previously advertised.

Michael Broad

Spacemutts: Attack of the Ninja Kittens!	978-0-330-51141-4	£4.99
Spacemutts: Fluffy Assassins from Mars!	978-0-330-51140-7	£4.99
Spacemutts: The Sausage Dog of Doom!	978-0-330-51142-1	£4.99

All Pan Macmillan titles can be ordered from our website, www.panmacmillan.com, or from your local bookshop and are also available by post from:

Bookpost, PO Box 29, Douglas, Isle of Man IM99 1BQ

Credit cards accepted. For details:
Telephone: 01624 677237
Fax: 01624 670923
Email: bookshop@enterprise.net
www.bookpost.co.uk

Free postage and packing in the United Kingdom